On My Way to Grandpa's

The Dial Press NEW YORK

On My Way to Grandpa's

by Ann Schweninger

Published by The Dial Press
1 Dag Hammarskjold Plaza
New York, New York 10017

Library of Congress
Cataloging in Publication Data

Schweninger, Ann.
On my way to Grandpa's.

Summary: Emily's trip to Grandpa's
house becomes a nature walk in the rain.
[1. Rain and rainfall—fiction.
2. Nature—Fiction] I. Title.
PZ7.S41263On   [E]   80-22729
ISBN 0-8037-6741-2
ISBN 0-8037-6752-8 (lib. bdg.)

To Mary

"Emily," said Mother, "take your
umbrella when you go to Grandpa's.
There's going to be a storm."

I sat on the porch and pulled
on my boots. The steps were still
warm from the sun.

But now the sky was full of clouds.

As I shut the front gate

I felt the first drop of rain.

I looked down. An ant was hurrying
up the side of his hill.

"Ant," I said, "inside your sand house
 you'll be warm and dry.
"I'll be cozy too at Grandpa's. He'll
 build a fire."

I reached out to touch the rain.

But the leaves above me caught
the drops.

High in a tree a squirrel peered
from his doorway.

He held a nut between his paws.
"Squirrel," I said, "that looks good!"

The breeze shook a branch, and rain

streamed in little rivers down my umbrella.

A mother bird sat on her nest.
Baby birds peeked out from
beneath her wings. The father bird
chirped a song.

"Birds," I said, "are you telling stories?
Grandpa tells me stories too."

Close by, a rabbit hid beneath a leaf. He
flattened his long ears to keep them
dry and nibbled clover blossoms.

"Don't worry, Rabbit," I said.
"Soon the sun will shine again.
Rain makes your clover grow."

Thunder rolled across the sky.
But I wasn't frightened.

I saw Grandpa's house at the
bottom of the hill.

Outside his gate my boots
squished in puddle mud.

I opened the gate and ran
up the walk.

"Grandpa!"

"Emily," he said, "come in and get dry.

"But before we go in, look!"

"A rainbow!" I said.

DATE DUE

MAR 25 '88			
JUN 15 '88			
JUL 13 '88			
1 9 JAN 1998			
6 FEB 1998			
2 6 MAR 1998			
1 6 JUN 1998			
GAYLORD			PRINTED IN U.S.A.